I0654833

John Dryden, Thomas Augustine Arne, Henry Purcell

The Songs, Airs, Duetts and Chorusses in the Masque of King Arthur

John Dryden, Thomas Augustine Arne, Henry Purcell

The Songs, Airs, Duetts and Chorusses in the Masque of King Arthur

ISBN/EAN: 9783337351168

Printed in Europe, USA, Canada, Australia, Japan

Cover: Foto ©Andreas Hilbeck / pixelio.de

More available books at **www.hansebooks.com**

THE
Songs, Airs, Duetts
and
Choruses
in the MASQUE of
KING ARTHUR
as Perform'd at the Theatre Royal in
DRURY LANE 4/
Compos'd by
Purcel & Dr Arne

Printed & Sold by IOHN IOHNSTON Nº 11. York Street COVENT GARDEN

Overture to King Arthur. *Compos'd by* Dr Arne.

Adapted for the HARPSICHORD by the Author.

Volti Presto.

Segue.

Largo.

The Side Drum MARCH.

End with the first Part.

Act 1st

Chorus. of Priests.

Purcel.

Sa.cri.fic'd, We have, We have, we have Sa.cri.fic'd.

Sa.crified. Wa have, we have, we have Sa.crified.

6   6   6 7   6 5 6 6 6   5 7
                                                            3 7

pia.

Mr Vernon.

Let Our next Obla.tion be to Thor thy Thun . . . . dring Son of such a.nother.

pia.
                                6   6   7   16   *   5 6
                                                    5 6

4.

We have Sa_cri_fic'd. We have fa_cri_fic'd. we have, we have, we have Sa_cri_fic'd.

We have Sa_cri_fic'd. we have Sa_cri_fic'd. we have we have we have Sa_cri_fic'd.

Mr Chámpnefs.

A Third, of Friezland breed was he, to Woden's wife & Thor's mother & now now now we

Duet.

Render thanks. thanks to Wo-den our de-fen-der. thanks. thanks thanks thanks to

Ren der thanks thanks. to Wo-den our de-fen der thanks. thanks. thanks. thanks to

thanks. thanks to Wo-den our de-fen-der thanks. thanks. thanks. thanks to

thanks thanks. to Wo-den our de-fen-der. thanks. thanks. thanks thanks to

Wo-den our de-fen der to Wo-den our de-fen-der.

Wo-den our de-fen-der to Wo-den our de-fen-der.

Segue Recit^e

Recitative, Mrs Scot.

The Lot is cast and Fan...fan pleas'd of mor.tal care   you shall you

shall.....be Eas'd   of mor.tal Care....you shall . . . . be

Eas'd.

Brave Souls to be renown'd in story to be renow'nd in sto—ry

Brave Souls to be renown'd in story to be renow'nd in sto—

Brave Souls to be renown'd in story to be renown'd in sto—ry to be re—

Brave Souls to

Violoncelli soli

tutti

Brave souls to be renown'd in sto—ry Brave souls to be renown'd in

———ry Brave souls to be renown'd in sto—ry to be renown'd in

nown'd renown'd in sto———ry to be renown'd renown'd in sto———ry

be renown'd in sto—ry Brave souls to be renown'd in sto—ry. Brave

Story to be renown'd in Sto..ry to be re-nown'd renown'd in Story

Story to be re-nown'd re...nown'd in Story

Brave Souls to be renown'd in Story to be renown'd in Story

Souls to be renown'd in Sto..ry to be re-nown'd renown'd in Story

Brave Souls to be renown'd in

Brave

ſtory to be re-now — — — — — — n'd in ſtory Brave

Souls to be renown'd in ſtory to be renown'd re-nown'd   in ſto-ry Brave

Brave Souls to be renown'd in ſtory to be renown'd in ſtory to be renown'd in

Brave Souls to be renown'd in ſtory to be renown'd in

Violoncelli Soli

Souls Brave Souls   to be renown'd in ſtory to be   renown'd renown'd in ſtory

Souls Brave Souls   to   be — — — renown'd renown'd in ſtory

ſto-ry to be renown'd in ſto-ry renown'd — to be renown'd in ſtory

ſtory renown'd in ſto — — ry to   be   renown'd renown'd — — renown'd in ſtory

Sung by Mr. Kear.

Allegro

I call I call I call you all to Wo_dens Hall your
temples rou _ _ _ _ _ _ nd with I _ vy bound in goblets Crown'd And
plenteous plenteous Bowls and plenteous plenteous Bowls of burnish'd Gold
Where ye shall Laugh and Dance and Quaff Where ye shall Laugh and Dance and Quaff the
Juice that makes the Britons Bold _ _ the Juice that makes the Britons Bold _ _
_ _ _ _ _ Where ye shall Laugh and Dance Where ye shall Laugh and Dance and
Quaff the Juice that makes the Juice that makes the Britons Bold the Juice that
makes the Juice that makes the Bri _ tons Bold. Segue il Coro

Chorus.

To Wodens Hall all all to Wodens Hall all all all all to Wodens Hall all all where in plenteous

To Wodens Hall all all to Wodens Hall all all all all to Wodens Hall all all where in plenteous

plenteous bowls of burnish'd Gold We shall laugh and dance and quaff we shall

We shall laugh and dance and quaff we shall laugh and dance shall

We shall laugh and dance and dance and quaff we shall laugh and

plenteous bowls of bur...nish'd gold. We shall laugh and dance and quaff the Juice that makes that

laugh and dance and quaff   we shall laugh and dance and quaff the Juice that makes   the

laugh and dance and quaff _ _ _ _   we shall laugh and quaff shall laugh and quaff _ _ _

dance   we shall laugh and dance _ _ _ _   and quaff   we shall laugh   and

makes the Britains bold _ _ _ _ _ _ _ _ _ _ _ _   we shall

Britains bold _ _ _ _ _ _ _ _ _   we shall laugh and dance shall

we shall laugh and quaff the Juice that makes the Britains

dance and quaff the Juice that makes   the Juice that makes   the Britains bold _ _ _ _ _ _

laugh and dance and quaff the Juice that makes that makes the Britains bold _ _ _ shall

Chorus of Warriors.

Oboe 1mo col Vio 1º

Oboe.

Vio 1º

Vio 2º

Viola.

Mr Vernon.

Basso.

Allegretto.

for.

pia.   for.   pia.

Come if you dare Our Trumpets sound, Come if you dare the Foes re-bound, We

pia   pias.   for

Come we come we come we come says the double double double beat of the thund'ring Drum.

Charge on a main now they Rally a gain the Gods from above the mad La bour be

hold and Pi ty Man kind that will Pe rish for Gold & pi ty Man kind that will Pe rish for

22.

Philidel.

Sung by Mˢ Baddeley.

Recit. accomp.

Andante.

....lafs. the Horrors of this bloody Field   Horrid it needs must be.

When I, a Spirit, can have so foft a fense of Human woes.   Ah.

For so many Souls as but this Day, were cloath'd with Flesh and warm'd with Vital

Blood.   But na. ked now.   Or Shir. ted but with Air.

Largo. *piaſ.*   Volti l'Aria.

AIR.

Larghet.

Oboe.

pia. for. pia.

O Peace.. De...scend.

juals;

Oboes.

To hu...man woes the Friend

Oh Charm to

Rest this troubled Isle, and o'er the Land Pro pi...tious smile.   thy smiles can chase these storms a.

...way... and darkest Night bring forth the Day... O Peace sweet Peace ap..pear... and plant thy o.live

here, and___ Plant thy O__live here. *pia.*

for   Oh Peace sweet Peace De___scend.   to

Hu__man woes the Freind.   O De__scend. to hu_man woes the Friend. thy

Smiles can chase these storms a_way,   from darkest Night bring forth the Day, O Peace sweet Peace ap

___pear and plant thy O__live here   and plant thy O___live here.   *for*

pia.   *for*

Air. Philidel.

Violino 1mo.

Violino 2do.

Mrs Baddeley.

pia

Andantino.

Hi-ther this way, Hi-ther this way, this way,

Bend, Trust not trust not. trust not that Ma-li-cious Fiend trust not that ma-li-cious

pia

Fiend Hi ther this way hi ther this way this way bend this way hi ther this way this way

for

Bend.

This way. hi_ther this way this way bend this way. hi_ther this way this way

This way. hi_ther this way this way bend this way. hi_ther this way this way

This way. this way hither this way this way bend. hi_ther this way hither this way

This way. this way hi_ther this way this way bend. hi_ther this way hi ther this way

pia.

Solo.

hi_ther this way this way bend If you ſtep no longer thinking, Down. . . . .

hither

this way

this way hi_ther this way this way bend.

You fall a furlong Sinking.

'Tis a Fiend who has An_noy'd ye Name but

Heav'n name but Heav'n and He'll a_void Ye, hi_ther this Way,

Turn to Pag

Fiend trust not that ma_li__cious Fiend. Hi__ther this way this way bend this way

Fiend Hi_ther this way this way bend this this way bend this way

Fiend Hi_ther this way this way bend.

Fiend trust not that ma_li__cious Fiend. Hi_ther this way this way

6   7 7 6 ᵇ   6ᵇ   6 * 6 7 6 * _ 6
4 3   4

this way.   hi_ther this way this way bend this way.   hi_ther this way this way Bend.

this way.   hi_ther.   bend this way.

this way   this way hi_ther.   this way hi ther

this way   this way hi_ther this way this way bend.   this way hi_ther this way this way Bend.

*   * 6 * 6   #6 * 6 6 *
5 5   5 5

Grimbald.   Mr. Bannister.

Andantino.

Let not a Moon born Elf mis lead ye from your Prey and from your Glo ry too far a lass he has be tray'd ye fol low the Flames that wave be fore Ye

Violino 1º

Violino 2º

sometimes Sev'n and sometimes One   Hur ry hur ry hurry hurry.   hur ry hur ry hur ry

Hur ry hur ry hurry On.

See the Footsteps plain appearing.
That way Oswald chose for flying,
Firm is the Turf and fit for bearing;
Where yonder pearly Dews are lying.
Far he cannot hence begone,
Hur ry hurry hurry on.

Philidel

Hi ther this way

Repeat the last Chorus from the S.

34

Philidel.　　　*Sung by* Mrs Baddeley.

Compos'd by Dr Arne on the Subject of Purcel's Chorus

Larghetto　P.　　Flutes　　Vio.　　Flutes

P: tasto

tutti

octaves

Come follow me come follow me　　and greenfword

P tasto

all your way fhall be　　come fol - - - - -

- - low me　　and greenfword all your way fhall be and greenfword all your way fhall be

F　P

tutti　　No Goblin or Elf fhall dare to offend ye no

Goblin or Elf fhall dare to offend we brethren of Air you Heroes will bear to the kind and the fair that at-

Chorus *Philidel's Party*

Sung by Mr Vernon

Di Arne.

O_ver our lowly sheds all the Storm paſses and when we die'tis in each others Arms in

each o_thers Arms in each o_thers Arms O_ver our lowly sheds all the Storm paſses O_ver our

lowly Shed all the Storm paſses and when we die. die. die. when we die'tis in Each o_thers

Arms in each o_thers Arms in each o_thersArms *for:* Flauti.

pia. *for:*

2.

Bright Nymphs of Britain, with Graces attended,
Let not your days without Pleasure expire;
Honor's but empty and when youth is ended,
All men will praise you but none will admire.
　　Let not youth fly away without contenting;
　　Age will come time enough for your repenting.

DUET.

Sung by Mrs Scot & Mrs Dorman.

Andantino

Sung by **Mrs Baddeley.**

Sung by **Mrs Baddeley.**

Dr. Arne

Recit.o Accomp.d

Thus thus thus I infuse these sov'reign

Dews ... fly back ye films that cloud her sight ... and you ye cryftal Humours

bright your noxious Vapours purg'd away. recover

and admit the Day tafto

now look abroad look abroad and fee all but me

Attendant Spirit. *Sung by* **Mrs Wrighten.**

Dr. Arne

Recit.o Accompanied

Oh Sight oh Sight the mother of defires what charming objects doft thou yeild! 'tis

fweet when tedious Night expires to fee the rofy Morning gild the mountain tops

Andante e pia

and paint the field

but when fair

Emm'line comes in fight   fhe makes the Summers day more bright

and when fhe goes a_way   when fhe goes   a_way   'tis Night.

Moderately quick

'Tis fweet 'tis

fweet the blufhing morn to view   and Plains adorn'd with pear._ly Dew   a_dorn'd   with pear._

Hoboy

_ly Dew but fuch cheap delights to fee fuch cheap delights   to fee   Heav'n and Nature give each

Symphony.

Air In the CHARACTER of Cupid. *Sung by* Mifs Rogers.

What Ho! what ho! thou Genius of this Isle. what ho, what ho . . . .

. . . What ho! Liest thou a sleep be-neath those hills of Snow, what ho, what ho, what ho, stretch out thy la-zy

slow.

Limbs, awake, awake, awake. and Winter from thy furry mantle shake. awake, awake & winter from thy furry mantle shake

faster.

In the CHARACTER of Winter. *Sung by* Mr Champnefs.

Vio. 1 mo.

Vio. 2º

Viola.

Winter

Slow.

What Pow'r art thou who from be_low hast made me

for

Rise un_willingly and Slow. from Beds of e...ver_last.....ingSnow.

53.

Seest thou not how stiff how stiff and wondrous Old, far far un.fit to bear the bit.ter Cold.

I can scarcely move or draw my Breath can scarcely move or draw my Breath   Let me

let me let me Freeze a gain.   let me let me Freeze a gain to Death let me let me let me freeze a gain to death.

Segue Presto.

Cupid.

MISS ROGERS.

Allegro. Thou doating Fool for..bear for..bear. what dost thou dream of freezing here. At Love s ap..pearing

all the Sky clearing the Stormy Winds their Fu..ry spare. Thou Doating Fool forbear for..bear. what dost thou

Dream of freezing here. Winter sub..duing and Spring re..new..ing my Beams cre..ate a more Glo..rious

Year thou Doating Fool for..bear for..bear. what dost thou dream of Freezing here.

Mr CHAMPNES.

Vio. 1.mo   pia.   for.   pia.

Vio. 2do.

Winter.

Great Love I know thee now eld..est of the Gods art thou.   Heav'n and

Slow.   pia   for.   pia.

Earth by thee were made Heav'n and Earth by thee were made. Hu..man Na..ture is thy Creature, Human

Nature is thy Creature. Ev_ry where, ev_ry where, every where, thou ar't thou ar't O_beyd.   Ev_ry where,

ev_ry where, ev_ry where, thou ar't thou ar't O_beyd. Ev_ry where thou art O_bey'd.

Cupid.

Recit: No Part of my Do_minion shall be waste to Spread . . . . my Sway. and

Sing . . . . my Praise. Ev'n Here, ev'n here, I will a People raise, of kind embra . . . . . . cing

Lo_vers and embrac'd. Ev'n here, ev'n here, I will a Peo_ple Raise of kind Em_bra_cing Lo_vers and em

. . brac'd.   Segue, Symphony.

Symphony *for the* Frost Scene.

Chorus.

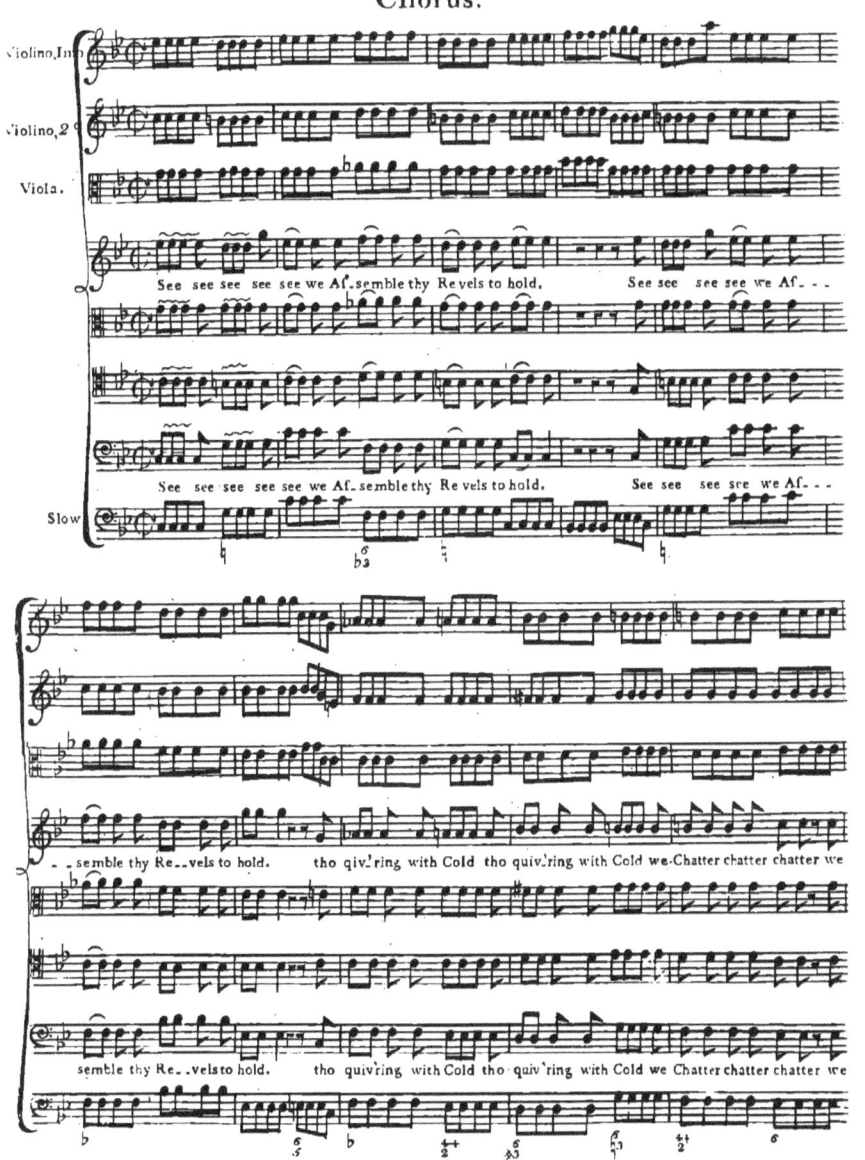

See see see see see we Af-semble thy Revels to hold.   See see see see we Af---

See see see see see we Af-semble thy Revels to hold.   See see see see we Af---

... semble thy Re...vels to hold.   tho qiv'ring with Cold tho quiv'ring with Cold we-Chatter chatter chatter we

semble thy Re...vels to hold.   tho quivring with Cold tho quiv'ring with Cold we Chatter chatter chatter we

Chatter chatter chatter we chatter chatter chatter and tremble. See see we af_semble thy Re_vels to

Chatter chatter chatter we chatter chatter chatter and tremble. See see we af_semble thy Re_vels to

Hold tho quiv'ring with Cold tho quiv'ring with Cold we Chatter chatter chatter we chatter chatter chatter and

Hold tho quiv'ring with Cold tho quiv'ring with Cold we Chatter chatter chatter we chatter chatter chatter and

Tremble See see see see we afsemble See see we af-semble thy Re-vels to hold.

Tremble See see see see we af-emble See see we af-semble thy Re-vels to hold.

Cupid.

Allo moderato

'Tis I.   'Tis I.   'Tis I   that have warm'd Ye, 'Tis I.   'Tis I.   'Tis

I that have warm'd Ye.   In spite of cold weather I've   Brought Ye to--gather.   'Tis I.   'Tis

I.   'Tis I   that have   warm'd Ye. 'Tis   I.   'Tis I.   'Tis I that have warmd Ye.

'Tis

'Tis

Love.   'Tis Love. 'Tis Love that has war m'd us.   'Tis Love. 'Tis Love. 'Tis Love that has warm'd us.

Love.   'Tis Love.'Tis Love that has warm'd us.   'Tis Love. 'Tis Love.'Tis Love that has warm'd us

Chorus.

'Tis Love. 'Tis Love. 'Tis Love that has

'Tis Love. 'Tis Love. 'Tis Love that has

Warm'd Us. 'Tis Love. 'Tis Love. 'Tis Love that has warm'd Us. In Spite of Cold Weather He's

Warm'd Us. 'Tis Love. 'Tis Love. 'Tis Love that has warm'd Us. In Spite of Cold Weather He's

In Spite of cold

In Spite of cold

weather He's brought us to-gether.   'Tis Love.   'Tis Love.   'Tis Love that has warm'd us.   'Tis

weather He's brought us to-gether.   'Tis Love.   'Tis Love.   'Tis Love that has warm'd us.   'Tis

Love. Tis Love. Tis Love that has warmd us.

Love. Tis Love. Tis Love that has warmd us.

End of the Third Act.

Act IV.

Siren's, Duet, *Sung by* Mrs Scot & Mi^ss Radley.

Mi^ss Radley

Two Daughters of this a..ged Stream are

Mrs Scot

Two Daughters of this a..ged Stream..are we. Two

Andante.

pia

Two Daughters of this A..ged Stream..........are

Daughters of this a..ged Stream are we. Two Daughters of this A..ged Stream are

we and both our Sea green locks have comb'd and both our Sea...green locks have comb'd have

we. and Both our Sea.green Locks have comb'd for Ye and both our Sea...green locks have

Comb'd for Ye. Come come come come Bathe with us an hour or two Come come

Comb'd for Ye. Come Come Bathe with Us an Hour or two Come Come

come come Na...ked in for we...are so What Dan..ger what Danger from a Na..ked

Come Come Na...ked in for We are so. what Dan..ger from a Na..ked

Nymphs and Sylvans.

Chorus.

Oboe, con Violini.

...co_ver He sighs not in vain. How sweet to dis_co_ver he sighs not in vain. the Lo_ver how Ea_sy his chain how

How hap_py

How hap_py the Lo_ver how ea_sy his chain how

Hap_py the Lov_er how pleasing his Pain. how sweet. how sweet to dis_cover he sighs not in

Hap_py the Lov_er how pleasing his Pain. how sweet. how sweet to dis_cover he sighs not in

Vain. How sweet· to dis_co_ver he Sighs not in Vain.

Vain. How sweet to dis__co_ver he sighs not in Vain.

Semi Chorus of Nymphs.

1st Nymph: In vain are our Graces in vain are your Eyes. In vain are our Graces if Love you des_pise.when age furrows

2d Nymph: In vain

3d Nymph: In vain are our Graces in vain are your Eyes. In vain are our Graces if Love you des_pise when age furrows

1st Sylvan:

2d Sylvan:

3d Sylvan:

Basso:

Allegro.non molto.

Faces 'tis too late to be wise 'tis too late too late 'tis 'tis too late to be wise.

Faces 'tis too late to be wise 'tis too late too late 'tis 'tis too late to be wise.

Chorus of Sylvans.

Then use the short Blefsing that

Then use the short Blefsing that

Flies in Pofsefsing that flies in pofsefsing No Joys no no no Joys are a-bove no joys are a-bove the Pleasures of

Flies in Pofsefsingthat Flies in Pofsefsing No Joys no no no Joys are a-bove no Joys are a-bove the Pleasures of

Chorus of Nymphs.

No no. no no. no no Joys are a-bove the Pleasures the Pleasures the Pleasures of Love.

No no. no no. no no Joys are a-bove the Pleasures the Pleasures the Pleasures of Love.

Love.

Love.

Love.

Segue il Coro.

Chorus.

No no.   no no.   no no Joys are a.bove the Pleasures the Pleasures the Pleasures of Love.

No no.   no no.   no Joys

No no.   no no.   no no Joys

No no   no no   no Joys are a. bove the Pleasures the Pleasures the Pleasures of Love.

for

Act V.

Eolus. *Sung by.* Mr. Champnefs.

Ye Blus___tring Bre___thren of ___ the Skies whose

Breath has Ruf...fled All the Wa...try Plain. Re...tire. Re...

tire. Re...tire. Re...tire and let Bri...tan...nia Rise........ Re...tire Retire and let Britannia Rise.

Tri......................umph O'er the Main.

Segue Subito.

Venus. *Sung by.* Mrs Scot.

Andantino

Fairest Isle all Isles Ex_cel_ling Seat _of Pleasures and of Love. Venus here will chuse her

Dwelling and for_sake her Cy_prian Grove. Cupid from his fav'rite Na_tion Care and En_vy

will re move Jealou_sy that Poy_sons Paf_sion and _Des_pair that Dies for Love.

Gen_tle Murmurs sweet com_plaings Sighs that blow the fire of Love. Soft Re_pul_ses

kind Dis_dai_ningshall be all the Pains you prove . Ev'_ry Swain shall pay his Du_ty

Grateful ev'ry Nymph shall prove And as these Ex_cell_in beauty those shall be re_nownd for Love.

Last Air and Chorus. Sung by Mr Vernon.

Allegro.

Sol_dier and a Saint. On this aus_pi_cious Order smile which Love and Arms, will plant will Plant

Sol_dier and a Saint.

Chorus.

for

for

On this Aus_pi_cious Or_der smile which Love and

On this Aus_pi_cious Or_der smile which Love and

for

Arms will Plant which Love and Arms will Plant. _low.

Arms will Plant which Love and Arms will Plant. _ low.

2ᵈ Verse.

Our Natives not alone appear,
To court this Martial Prize;
But foreign Kings, adopted here,
Their Crowns at home despise.

3ᵈ Verse.

Our Sov'reign high, in awful State,
His Honours shall bestow;
And see his Scepter'd Subjects wait,
On his Commands Below.

CountryDance. end of the 3ᵈ Act. Mʳ Dibdin.

MARCH, for the Entry of the WARRIORS.

FINE.